Unknown vs Satan

Control Of Hells Realm

Bradley T. Livingston

Copyright © 2024

Bradley T. Livingston

Ebook ISBN: 978-1-965064-43-6

Paperback ISBN: 978-1-965064-44-3

Hardback ISBN : 978-1-965064-45-0

All Rights Reserved. Any unauthorized reprint or use of this material is strictly prohibited. No part of this book may be reproduced or transmitted in any form or by any means, electronic or mechanical, including photocopying, recording, or by any information storage and retrieval system without express written permission from the author.

All reasonable attempts have been made to verify the accuracy of the information provided in this publication. Nevertheless, the author assumes no responsibility for any errors and/or omissions.

About the Author

Bradley T. Livingston, a 12.5-year veteran of the U.S. Army and Army National Guard, seeks to inspire the global community through his unique approach to horror #ChildrensStories.

Additionally, he is launching a novel online homeschooling alternative, prioritizing the convenience of home-based learning and fostering a secure educational setting for students.

This educational initiative is identified as Bradley T. Livingston High School College and Bradley T. Livingston High School for the Arts, serving as the home of the Taipans.

Dedication

"To you, dear reader, for making this journey worthwhile."

"For my readers, who breathe life into these pages."

"To all those who pick up this book, thank you for giving my words a chance."

"For every reader who finds a piece of themselves within these chapters."

In loving memory to my grandmother Pearlie Mae Mumford 1932-2021

Acknowledgment

My mother is an amazing woman. I find it difficult to say what she means to me in just a few sentences. I thank my mom for bringing me into this world; no other gift can bear. I was disciplined by this woman named Virgie Mae Saunders (Stoner) and a grandmother named Pearlie Mae Mumford, who taught me right from wrong each and every day to make something out of my life (Psalms 19:1; Romans 1:20).

Contents

Dedication i

Acknowledgment ii

About the Author iii

UNKNOWN VS SATAN

The challenging part about dealing with a Temporary Restraining Order (TRO) is that while it is serious, probation takes it to another level. Probation often comes with multiple requirements such as weekly meetings, anger management classes, various other meetings, a strict no weapons policy, no drugs or alcohol, and the possibility of random testing. Additionally, there are usually mandatory monthly check-ins with a parole officer. All these requirements come at your own expense, and the authorities are indifferent to how disruptive these obligations might be to your job or daily life.

Giving a false statement to any law enforcement entity is considered a crime, whether the statement is sworn or unsworn. However, in practical terms, such offenses are rarely prosecuted. Restraining orders or protection from abuse orders are often misused by many individuals for reasons unrelated to actual safety concerns. Unfortunately, the people who genuinely need these protections often find themselves inadequately protected. Those who abuse the system do so to cause harm rather than to seek protection.

I have observed this issue from both perspectives. There are individuals who are genuinely harmed and left holding a piece of paper that offers no real protection. On the other hand, there are those who use that same piece of paper as a weapon of mass destruction, manipulating the system to their advantage. The system is fundamentally flawed and requires significant reforms to protect the rights and well-being of all parties involved.

One of the most effective ways to deal with a narcissist is to walk away from them. Narcissists are often unable to recognize their own narcissism and are more shocked and offended when someone chooses to leave their sphere of influence. A narcissist's most common trait is an inflated sense of self-importance, which I have frequently observed in my experiences.

Proverbs 31:10-12

A wife of noble character who can find? She is worth far more than rubies. Her husband has full confidence in her and lacks nothing of value. She brings him good, not harm, all the days of her life.

Ecclesiastes 4:9-12

Two are better than one because they have a good return for their labor: If either of them falls down, one can help the other up. But pity anyone who falls and has no one to help them up. Also, if two lie down together, they will keep warm. But how can one keep warm alone? Though one may be overpowered, two can defend themselves. A cord of three strands is not quickly broken.

Mark 10:6-9

But at the beginning of creation God 'made them male and female.' 'For this reason, a man will leave his father and mother and be united to his wife, and the two will become one flesh.' So they are no longer two, but one flesh. Therefore what God has joined together, let no one separate.

Love Your Enemies

Psalm 35:11-14

UNKNOWN VS SATAN

Malicious witnesses rise up; they ask me of things that I do not know. They repay me evil for good; my soul is bereft. But I, when they were sick, wore sackcloth; I afflicted myself with fasting; I prayed with my head bowed on my chest. I went about as though I grieved for my friend or my brother; as one who laments his mother, I bowed down in mourning.

In this passage, the psalmist speaks of being falsely accused and mistreated by malicious witnesses. Despite the evil done to him, he describes how he responded with compassion and empathy when his adversaries were in trouble. He wore sackcloth, fasted, and prayed for them as if they were his own family, demonstrating a profound commitment to loving one's enemies even in the face of wrongdoing.

Proverbs 10:12

Hatred stirs up strife, but love covers all offenses.

This proverb highlights the destructive nature of hatred and the healing power of love. Hatred leads to conflict and discord, while love has the ability to forgive and mend relationships. By choosing love over hatred, we can prevent strife and create a more peaceful and harmonious environment.

Matthew 5:44

Love your enemies and pray for those who persecute you, so that you may be sons of your Father who is in heaven.

In this verse, Jesus instructs us to love our enemies and pray for those who persecute us. This teaching challenges us to rise above our natural inclinations for revenge and instead show compassion and love. By doing so, we reflect the character of our Heavenly Father and demonstrate our true identity as His children.

Luke 6:27

But I say to you who hear, Love your enemies, do good to those who hate you, bless those who curse you, pray for those who abuse you.

Jesus emphasizes the importance of loving our enemies and doing good to those who hate us. He calls us to bless those who curse us and pray for those who mistreat us. This radical approach to love transforms our relationships and can potentially change the hearts of those who oppose us.

Luke 6:35

But love your enemies, and do good, and lend, expecting nothing in return, and your reward will be great, and you will be sons of the Most High, for he is kind to the ungrateful and the evil.

Here, Jesus encourages us to love our enemies, do good, and lend without expecting anything in return. By doing so, we will receive a great reward and be recognized as children of the Most High God, who shows kindness even to the ungrateful and the wicked. This teaching reminds us of the boundless nature of God's love and challenges us to emulate it in our own lives.

Romans 12:20-21

On the contrary, "If your enemy is hungry, feed him; if he is thirsty, give him something to drink; for by so doing you will heap burning coals on his head." Do not be overcome by evil, but overcome evil with good.

The apostle Paul instructs us to respond to our enemies with kindness and generosity. By meeting their needs, we can potentially cause them to reflect on their actions and experience remorse. Paul urges us not to be overcome by evil but to overcome evil with good, highlighting the transformative power of love and kindness.

Ephesians 3:14-19

For this reason, I bow my knees before the Father, from whom every family in heaven and on earth is named, that according to the riches of his glory he may grant you to be strengthened with power through his Spirit in your inner being, so that Christ may dwell in your hearts through faith—that you, being rooted and grounded in love, may have strength to comprehend with all the saints what is the breadth and length and height and depth, and to know the love of Christ that surpasses knowledge, that you may be filled with all the fullness of God.

In this prayer, Paul expresses his desire for believers to be strengthened by the Holy Spirit and to have Christ dwell in their hearts through faith. He prays that they may be deeply rooted and grounded in love, enabling them to understand the vastness of Christ's love, which surpasses all knowledge. By experiencing this profound love, believers can be filled with the fullness of God, empowering them to love others, including their enemies, in the same way Christ loves us.

Philippians 1:9-11

And it is my prayer that your love may abound more and more, with knowledge and all discernment, so that you may approve what is excellent, and so be pure and blameless for the day of Christ, filled with the fruit of righteousness that comes through Jesus Christ, to the glory and praise of God.

2 Thessalonians 3:5

May the Lord lead your hearts into a full understanding and expression of the love of God and the patient endurance that comes from Christ.

Jesus Christ will appear in power and glory at the end of the tribulation and destroy the lawless, the antichrist. Jesus will bring judgment upon all unbelievers and usher in His worldwide rule during the Millennium when believers will rule and reign with Him.

God has not revealed to us all the details of His prophetic timeline. Anyone who has studied prophecy seriously must be humble, realizing that there are still many unanswered questions. God has not promised to answer all our questions about the future. However, we know enough to be encouraged and live our lives for Him in these last days.

What's the take-home message in this prophetic timeline?

Evil and lawlessness are going to continue to increase. However, believers filled with the Holy Spirit are the restraining power that holds back this evil and lives as witnesses for Jesus in these last days. No matter how bad evil may get in our lives or our country, we know the end of the story. One day, Jesus will come to take us home. He will judge all evil and we will live with Him forever and ever.

Trust in God's Protection

2 Thessalonians 2:13 (NIV)

"But we ought always to thank God for you, brothers loved by the Lord, because from the beginning God chose you to be saved through the sanctifying work of the Spirit and through belief in the truth."

The Lord loves you. He chose you to be saved. The Holy Spirit lives inside of you and you believe in the truth of God's Word. As you follow Jesus, you will not be deceived.

2 Thessalonians 2:14-15 (NIV)

"He called you to this through our gospel, that you might share in the glory of our Lord Jesus Christ. So then, brothers, stand firm and hold to the teachings we passed on to you, whether by word of mouth or by letter."

Those who stand firm are destined to share in the glory of Jesus Christ at the end of time. Whatever you are going through today, God wants you to stand firm in faith.

2 Thessalonians 2:16-17 (NIV)

"May our Lord Jesus Christ himself and God our Father, who

loved us and by his grace gave us eternal encouragement and good hope, encourage your hearts and strengthen you in every good deed and word."

God wants you to be encouraged this morning and strengthened. You need strength to do the good deeds and speak the good words that God has planned for you this week. Receive God's encouragement.

If you're a believer here this morning, you're a soldier of the kingdom of God. You are at war with the kingdom of darkness. In the last days, the conflict will increase in fierceness, and evil will grow worse. Yet many will be won to the kingdom of God by those who stand firm to the end. God wants you to be encouraged and to be an encourager to others. Will you commit with me to stand firm on God's Word during these last days? Together we can see God do great things through our lives and through our church. Let your light shine, drive back the darkness, and overcome evil with good.

What does "Jesus was a radical" mean?

What sort of radical do Christians believe Jesus was? Loving, merciful, caring, non-violent, fair, self-sacrificing, and just. He helped people who were normally ignored; this was radical: He ate with tax collectors and sinners, saying, "Healthy people don't need a doctor, sick people do."

The Bible reveals that every single human being—young, old, rich, and poor, born and unborn, black and white—is made in the image of God (Genesis 1:27). Therefore, every single human is equally worthy of dignity, value, and respect as an image-bearer of God.

The Apostle Paul said, "[God] made from one man every nation of mankind to live on all the face of the earth" (Acts 17:26). The beautiful, diverse, multi-hued tapestry of humanity is God's idea. Racial distinctiveness is meant to showcase God's immeasurable creativity and boundless originality.

Jesus came as a Middle Eastern man. God-incarnate was brown. When He returns again, His redeemed people will be comprised of a countless multitude, "from every nation, from all tribes and peoples and languages" (Rev. 7:9). In a word, God's saving purposes in the world, in Jesus, are multi-ethnic.

Evil and the Supernatural

The concept of evil is often associated with supernatural powers or creatures, especially in fictional and religious contexts. The monsters of fiction, such as vampires, witches, and werewolves, are thought to be paradigms of evil. These creatures possess powers and abilities that defy scientific explanation, and perhaps human understanding. Many popular horror films also depict evil as the result of dark forces or Satanic possession.

Evil and Explanatory Power

The concept of evil would have explanatory power, or be explanatorily useful, if it were able to explain why certain actions were performed or why these actions were performed by certain agents rather than by others. Evil sceptics such as Inga Clendinnen and Philip

Cole argue that the concept of evil cannot provide explanations of this sort and thus should be abandoned. They believe that labeling actions or individuals as evil does not help us understand the underlying causes or motivations behind those actions. Instead, they suggest that we should focus on more precise and detailed explanations that take into account psychological, social, and environmental factors.

The Dangers of 'Evil'

Some evil-skeptics believe that we should abandon the concept of evil because it is too harmful or dangerous to use. No one can deny that the term 'evil' can be harmful or dangerous when it is misapplied, used perniciously, or used without sensitivity to complicated historical or political contexts. The label of 'evil' has often been used to dehumanize or demonize individuals or groups, leading to further conflict and suffering. By attributing actions to 'evil,' we may oversimplify complex situations and ignore the broader context that may have contributed to those actions. This can result in unjust policies, discrimination, and even violence against those labeled as 'evil.'

The Concept of Divine Love

God was motivated by love to save the world (John 3:16). God's love is best seen in the sacrifice of Christ on our behalf (1 John 4:9). And God's love does not require us to be "worthy" to receive it; His love is truly benevolent and gracious: "God demonstrates his own love for us in this: While we were still sinners, Christ died for us" (Romans 5:8). True love is part of God's nature, and God is the source of love. He is the initiator of a loving relationship with us. Any love we have for God is simply a response to His sacrificial love for us: "This is love: not that we loved God, but that he loved us and sent his Son as an atoning sacrifice for our sins" (1 John 4:10). Our human understanding of love is flawed, weak, and incomplete, but the more we look at Jesus, the better we understand true love.

God's love for us in Christ has resulted in our being brought into His family: "See what great love the Father has lavished on us, that we should be called children of God! And that is what we are!" (1 John 3:1). A different situation exists with what some call "evil" that they see in natural and historical events. When God says, "I create evil" (Isa. 45:7, KJV), He is not referring to moral evil (Jas. 1:13-15) but to the destruction under His control in nature or in history. Instead of the word "evil," the NKJV and the ESV read "calamity." The NASB reads "disaster" and the NRSV reads "woe." There is only one God, and everything is completely under His control. He created nature and natural forces and the way they operate (Gen. 1). Just as the father in the parable showed love to his prodigal son (Luke 15:11-32), so our Heavenly Father receives us with joy when we come to Him in faith. He makes us "accepted in the Beloved" (Ephesians 1:6, NKJV).

"For this is the love of God, that we keep His commandments: and His commandments are not burdensome" (1 John 5:3; cf. John 14:15). We serve God out of love for Him. God's love for us enables us to obey Him freely, without the burden of guilt or the fear of punishment. "There is no fear in love, but perfect love casts out fear. Fear has to do with punishment, and whoever fears has not been perfected in love" (1 John 4:18).

"I love those who love me, and those who seek me diligently find me" (Proverbs 8:17). God's steadfast love is unfailing: "For the mountains may depart and the hills be removed, but my steadfast love shall not depart from you, and my covenant of peace shall not be removed," says the Lord, who has compassion on you" (Isaiah 54:10).

"For God so loved the world, that He gave His only Son, that whoever believes in Him should not perish but have eternal life" (John 3:16). "I have been crucified with Christ. It is no longer I who live, but Christ who lives in me. And the life I now live in the flesh I live by faith in the Son of God, who loved me and gave Himself for me" (Galatians 2:20).

"But the fruit of the Spirit is love, joy, peace, patience, kindness, goodness, faithfulness, gentleness, self-control; against such things, there is no law" (Galatians 5:22-23). "You shall not take vengeance or bear a grudge against the sons of your own people, but you shall love your neighbor as yourself: I am the Lord" (Leviticus 19:18).

"Whoever covers an offense seeks love, but he who repeats a matter separates close friends" (Proverbs 17:9). "A friend loves at all times, and a brother is born for adversity" (Proverbs 17:17).

A true friend loves at all times, and a brother is there for you in times of adversity. This is a profound truth that highlights the importance of unwavering support and loyalty among friends and family.

UNKNOWN VS SATAN

Matthew 7:12 teaches us a fundamental principle: "So whatever you wish that others would do to you, do also to them, for this is the Law and the Prophets." This verse encapsulates the essence of empathy and mutual respect. Treating others as we would like to be treated creates a foundation of kindness and understanding.

In John 13:34-35, we are given a new commandment: "A new commandment I give to you, that you love one another: just as I have loved you, you also are to love one another. By this, all people will know that you are my disciples, if you have love for one another." This directive emphasizes the importance of love and how it serves as a distinguishing mark of true discipleship.

John 15:12-13 reinforces this commandment: "This is my commandment, that you love one another as I have loved you. Greater love has no one than this, that someone lay down his life for his friends." This verse underscores the profound depth of love, highlighting the ultimate sacrifice one can make for their friends.

Romans 12:9-10 encourages genuine love: "Let love be genuine. Abhor what is evil; hold fast to what is good. Love one another with brotherly affection. Outdo one another in showing honor." True love is sincere and unselfish, striving to honor others above oneself.

Romans 13:8-10 speaks to the power of love in fulfilling the law: "Owe no one anything, except to love each other, for the one who loves another has fulfilled the law. For the commandments, 'You shall not commit adultery, You shall not murder, You shall not steal, You shall not covet,' and any other commandment, are summed up in this word: 'You shall love your neighbor as yourself.' Love does no wrong to a neighbor; therefore love is the fulfilling of the law." Love is the foundation of moral conduct, encapsulating all commandments through the simple act of loving one another.

1 Corinthians 16:14 offers a concise yet powerful directive: "Let all that you do be done in love." Every action, no matter how small, should be motivated by love.

Galatians 5:13-14 reminds us of the freedom and responsibility we have: "For you were called to freedom, brothers. Only do not use your freedom as an opportunity for the flesh, but through love serve one another. For the whole law is fulfilled in one word: 'You shall love your neighbor as yourself.'" True freedom is found in serving others with love, not indulging in selfish desires.

Ephesians 4:1-3 calls us to live a life worthy of our calling: "I therefore, a prisoner for the Lord, urge you to walk in a manner worthy of the calling to which you have been called, with all humility and gentleness, with patience, bearing with one another in love, eager to maintain the unity of the Spirit in the bond of peace." Humility, gentleness, and patience are essential in maintaining unity and peace among believers.

Ephesians 4:32 encourages kindness and forgiveness: "Be kind to one another, tenderhearted, forgiving one another, as God in Christ forgave you." Kindness and forgiveness are reflections of God's love and mercy towards us.

Philippians 2:1-4 calls for unity and humility: "So if there is any encouragement in Christ, any comfort from love, any participation in the Spirit, any affection and sympathy, complete my joy by being of the same mind, having the same love, being in full accord and of one mind. Do nothing from selfish ambition or conceit, but in humility count others more significant than yourselves. Let each of you look not only to his own interests but also to the interests of others." Unity and humility are achieved by valuing others above ourselves and seeking their well-being alongside our own.

Colossians 3:12-14 instructs us on the virtues we should embrace: "Put on then, as God's chosen ones, holy and beloved, compassionate hearts, kindness, humility, meekness, and patience, bearing with one another and, if one has a complaint against another, forgiving each other; as the Lord has forgiven you, so you also must forgive. And above all these put on love, which binds everything together in perfect harmony." This passage encourages us to cultivate compassion, kindness, humility, gentleness, and patience. It also highlights the importance of forgiveness, reminding us that we should forgive others just as the Lord has forgiven us. Above all, we are urged to embrace love, which unifies and perfects all other virtues.

James 2:8 reinforces the importance of love in our actions: "If you really fulfill the royal law according to the Scripture, 'You shall love your neighbor as yourself,' you are doing well." This verse calls us to live out the royal law of love, treating others with the same care and respect that we would wish for ourselves.

1 Peter 1:22 emphasizes sincere love: "Having purified your

souls by your obedience to the truth for a sincere brotherly love, love one another earnestly from a pure heart." This verse encourages us to love one another genuinely and deeply, with a pure heart.

1 Peter 4:8 highlights the power of love: "Above all, keep loving one another earnestly, since love covers a multitude of sins." Love is powerful and transformative, capable of overcoming many wrongs.

1 John 3:16-18 defines true love through action: "By this, we know love, that he laid down his life for us, and we ought to lay down our lives for the brothers. But if anyone has the world's goods and sees his brother in need, yet closes his heart against him, how does God's love abide in him? Little children, let us not love in word or talk but in deed and in truth." This passage calls us to demonstrate our love through self-sacrifice and practical support for those in need.

1 John 4:7 reminds us that love is a reflection of God's nature: "Beloved, let us love one another, for love is from God, and whoever loves has been born of God and knows God." True love originates from God, and those who love others show that they belong to Him.

1 John 4:19 explains the source of our love: "We love because he first loved us." Our ability to love comes from God's initial love for us.

Ephesians 5:25 instructs husbands to love their wives: "Husbands love your wives, as Christ loved the church and gave himself up for her." This verse sets a high standard for marital love, comparing it to Christ's sacrificial love for the church.

Ephesians 5:33 calls for mutual respect in marriage: "However, let each one of you love his wife as himself, and let the wife see that she respects her husband." Love and respect are essential components of a healthy and balanced relationship.

A champion is more than just a winner; a champion is an upholder, an advocate, a defender, a supporter, and someone who speaks up for a cause. In Psalm 89:19-20, we see a promise of hope through the raising up of a champion: "I have found a champion. I have found David among the people; I have anointed him." This champion will be victorious over enemies, bringing hope and triumph.

2 Timothy 4:7 reflects on a life of faithful endurance: "I have fought the good fight, I have finished the course, I have kept the faith." This verse speaks to the perseverance and steadfastness required to complete our spiritual journey.

Isaiah 5:22 offers a cautionary note: "How terrible it will be for those who are heroes at drinking wine, and champions in mixing strong drinks." This verse warns against the dangers of excessive indulgence and the false sense of heroism it can bring.

Psalm 89:19 also speaks of God's provision of a champion: "Once You spoke in a vision to Your godly ones, And said, 'I have given help to one who is mighty [giving him the power to be a champion for Israel]; I have exalted one chosen from the people.'" God empowers and raises up champions for His purposes.

Isaiah 42:13-17 portrays the Lord as a mighty champion: "The LORD will march out like a champion, like a warrior he will stir up his zeal; with a shout he will raise the battle cry and will triumph over his enemies. For a long time I have kept silent, I have been quiet and held myself back. But now, like a woman in childbirth, I cry out, gasp and pant. I will lay waste the mountains and hills and dry up all their vegetation; I will turn rivers into islands and dry up the pools. I will lead the blind by ways they have not known, along unfamiliar paths I will guide them; I will turn the darkness into light before them and make the rough places smooth. These are the things I will do; I will not forsake them. But those who trust in idols, who say to images, 'You are our gods,' will be turned back in utter shame." This passage vividly describes the Lord's power and determination to lead and protect His people, transforming obstacles and guiding them through challenges while also warning against the futility of idolatry.

Isaiah 42:13-17 is a prophecy concerning the Messiah, portrayed as the servant of the Lord and His chosen one. The Messiah is described as someone whom God supports and with whom He is well pleased. The passage highlights that the Messiah is uniquely qualified for His work by being endowed with the Spirit without measure. Isaiah 42:1 introduces this servant and emphasizes his divine support and the pleasure God takes in him. The Messiah's humility and meekness are portrayed in Isaiah 42:2, indicating that he would not shout or raise his voice in public. Instead, he would carry out his mission quietly and without seeking attention.

Isaiah 42:3 further illustrates the Messiah's tender nature, depicting him as someone who would not break a bruised reed or extinguish a faintly burning wick. This imagery signifies his compassion and gentleness towards those who are weak and ignorant. Despite his meekness, Isaiah 42:4 describes his courage and resolution, affirming that he will not falter or be discouraged until he establishes justice on earth.

The prophecy continues with the Messiah's call to His work and the different aspects of it. This is introduced by emphasizing the greatness of God who called Him. God is portrayed as the Creator of the heavens and the earth and of all the people on it (Isaiah 42:5-7). His name is Jehovah, a name that signifies His eternal and self-existing nature. God's glory is unique and incommunicable to any creature, and His knowledge extends to future events, which are predicted by Him (Isaiah 42:8-9).

The Gentiles are then called to praise the Lord and give Him glory. This call to praise is partly due to the promises concerning the Messiah (Isaiah 42:10-12) and partly due to the destruction of God's enemies (Isaiah 42:13-15). Moreover, God's gracious care for those who were previously blind and ignorant is highlighted in Isaiah 42:16. He promises to lead them by paths they have not known, turning darkness into light and making rough places smooth. These actions underscore God's commitment to not forsake His people.

Isaiah 42:17-18 prophesies the confusion and downfall of idolaters, urging them to seek true knowledge and light. The blindness, ignorance, and stubbornness of the Jews are exposed, yet a remnant among them remains with whom the Lord is pleased, for the sake of the righteousness of His Son (Isaiah 42:19-21). However, the majority of the people will face consequences for their sins and disobedience, becoming victims of divine wrath and vengeance (Isaiah 42:22-24).

Moral "evil" is that which is opposed to God. It is the opposite of God's nature and contrary to His will. Evil does not exist as an independent entity but in relation to God and good. All goodness originates in God and comes from Him. Anything that opposes God is evil. Evil denies God's existence or contradicts and perverts His words.

Moral evil is essentially disobeying God and the consequences that follow such disobedience. Jesus referred to "the evil one" in Matthew 6:13, indicating that there is a spiritual being who is the mastermind and driving force behind all moral evil. This being is known as Satan, also called "the devil," as seen in the temptation of Jesus in Matthew 4:1-11. Satan is the one who brought destruction to the family of the righteous man Job and inflicted pain and misery on him (Job 1-2).

Before the creation of the heavens and the earth, an angel rebelled against God's leadership and led a group of other angels in opposition to God's will. These evil beings are referred to when the Apostle Paul wrote that Jesus Christ is seated in the heavenly places "far above every ruler and authority, power and dominion, and every title given" (Ephesians 1:21). Paul also wrote that "our struggle is not against flesh and blood, but against the rulers, against the authorities, against the cosmic powers of this darkness, against evil, spiritual forces in the heavens" (Ephesians 6:12). The Apostle Peter stated that Jesus "has gone into heaven and is at the right hand of God with angels, authorities, and powers subject to Him" (1 Peter 3:22). This evil being is our adversary who "is prowling around like a roaring lion, looking for anyone he can devour" (1 Peter 5:8). Eventually, Satan and all his evil cohorts will be destroyed by God (Revelation 21:10).

God is not the author of evil. He cannot be tempted by evil, nor does He tempt anyone to do evil (James 1:13). Satan is the ultimate source of all moral evil. Jesus called him "a murderer from the beginning" and "the father of all liars" (John 8:44). But where does evil within us or by us originate? James provides the answer: "Each person is tempted when he is lured and enticed by his own desire. Then desire, when it has conceived, gives birth to sin, and sin, when it is fully grown, brings forth death" (James 1:14-15). Sin is disobedience to God. It manifests in our actions, words, and thoughts that are contrary to God's will.

In summary, Isaiah 42:13-17 and the surrounding verses offer a rich prophecy about the Messiah, His mission, and His character. They highlight God's greatness, the call to the Gentiles to praise Him, the downfall of idolaters, and His care for the blind and ignorant. The passage also connects to the broader theological discussion of moral evil, its origins, and its ultimate defeat by God. Moral evil, rooted in opposition to God, is driven by Satan but can also arise from our own desires. The ultimate resolution of this evil is found in the person and work of the Messiah, who embodies God's love and justice.

In understanding the concept of "evil" as it relates to natural and historical events, it's crucial to differentiate it from moral evil, which involves disobedience to God's will and harmful actions against others. The phrase from Isaiah 45:7 in the King James Version, where God says, "I create evil," has been a topic of debate and misunderstanding. In other translations like the NKJV and ESV, the word "evil" is rendered as "calamity," while the NASB uses "disaster," and the NRSV uses "woe." These variations clarify that God's statement refers to calamitous events or disasters under His control within the natural and historical order, not moral evil.

God, being the creator of all things, including nature and its forces, established the laws that govern them (Genesis 1). Natural phenomena such as storms, hurricanes, and tornadoes are part of the functioning of these created natural laws. While these events can cause destruction and loss of life, they are distinct from moral evil because they are not driven by moral agency or intent to disobey God's moral standards.

Jesus himself acknowledged the impartiality of natural forces in Matthew 5:45, stating that the sun rises and the rain falls on both the righteous and the unrighteous alike. This universal impact of natural occurrences underscores their indiscriminate nature in affecting everyone, regardless of their moral standing.

Biblical narratives illustrate how both ordinary people and followers of God have encountered and been affected by natural forces. For instance, Jesus' disciples faced a life-threatening storm on the Sea of Galilee (Matthew 14:23-33), and the Apostle Paul endured a perilous storm in the Mediterranean Sea (Acts 27). In these situations, God's sovereignty over nature is evident, whether through miraculous intervention or through the natural order He has established.

Since the fall of Adam and Eve in the Garden of Eden (Genesis 3), humanity and the entire created order have been subject to decay and suffering (Romans 5:12-21). This fallen state includes the vulnerability of nature itself to degradation and destruction until the final redemption when Jesus returns (Romans 8:19-23). At that time, Jesus will defeat Satan and all forces of evil, ushering in a new era described as "the new heavens and the new earth," where death and decay will cease to exist (2 Peter 3:13; Revelation 21:1-8).

While natural disasters and historical calamities may cause immense suffering and loss, they do not constitute moral evil as understood in biblical terms. They operate within the framework of natural laws established by God and affect all people universally. The ultimate resolution of all forms of evil, whether moral or natural, is found in the redemptive work of Jesus Christ, who will ultimately restore and renew creation to its intended perfection.

Unknown The Slasher

In the midst of a thunderstorm on a dark, eerie night, a scene of horrific brutality unfolds. Slave masters, driven by cruelty and malice, unleash unimaginable torment upon their helpless slaves. The air is thick with fear and desperation as cries of pain echo through the hollow ground. Slaves are subjected to relentless punishment, their bodies bearing the scars of lashings that tear through flesh and draw blood.

Amidst this scene of terror, a figure emerges unexpectedly —

UNKNOWN THE SLASHER. With lightning speed and ferocious anger, he strikes out against the oppressors. In a swift and violent act, he decapitates one slave owner and consumes the heart of another with his razor-sharp claws. The slaves, witnessing this unexpected intervention, are shaken to their core, terrified yet oddly comforted by the slasher's relentless pursuit of justice.

UNKNOWN THE SLASHER, fueled by a deep-seated rage against injustice, has amassed a formidable tally of victims. As he approaches his thousandth kill, even the malevolent forces that have tormented him in the past begin to take notice. He sets his sights on a new target — Satan himself, the embodiment of all evil and suffering.

In a moment of reflection, UNKNOWN THE SLASHER's grandmother appears, urging caution and restraint. She reminds him of Satan's power to manipulate and deceive, warning him of the dangers ahead. Despite her plea, UNKNOWN THE SLASHER is resolute in his mission to eradicate evil from the world and imprison wrongdoers in hell's eternal grasp.

Memories of personal tragedy fuel UNKNOWN THE SLASHER's determination. He recalls the suffering inflicted upon his family by demonic forces, including the tragic loss of his uncle. These memories strengthen his resolve to confront Satan head-on, regardless of the risks involved.

Steeling himself for the ultimate confrontation, UNKNOWN THE SLASHER enters through an ominous elevator door marked with the chilling inscription "SATAN." As he pushes forward into

UNKNOWN VS SATAN

hell's fiery domain, he envisions Satan seated upon his dark throne, reigning over a realm of unimaginable torment and despair.

SATAN

MUZAN

UNKNOWN VS SATAN

In the heart of hell's fiery domain, UNKNOWN THE SLASHER stands at the threshold of a monumental battle. With unwavering determination, he pushes the button on the ominous elevator, knowing he may never return unless Satan is defeated. The path before him is treacherous, lined with crumbled red rocks and pools of molten fire that blaze and roar around him.

As UNKNOWN THE SLASHER confronts Satan on his dark throne, the ruler of hell challenges his presence. Satan, aware of the slasher's intent, taunts him with defiance, claiming nothing can sway his malevolent purpose. Undeterred, UNKNOWN THE SLASHER's claws begin to sharpen and grow, a sign of his readiness for the impending clash.

A tense standoff ensues, and suddenly, UNKNOWN THE SLASHER begins to vanish like dust, leaving Satan momentarily bewildered. In a swift and decisive move, UNKNOWN THE SLASHER reappears with ferocity, tearing out Satan's eyes one by one. With each act of brutality, the once-powerful Satan weakens, his evil grip over hell slipping away.

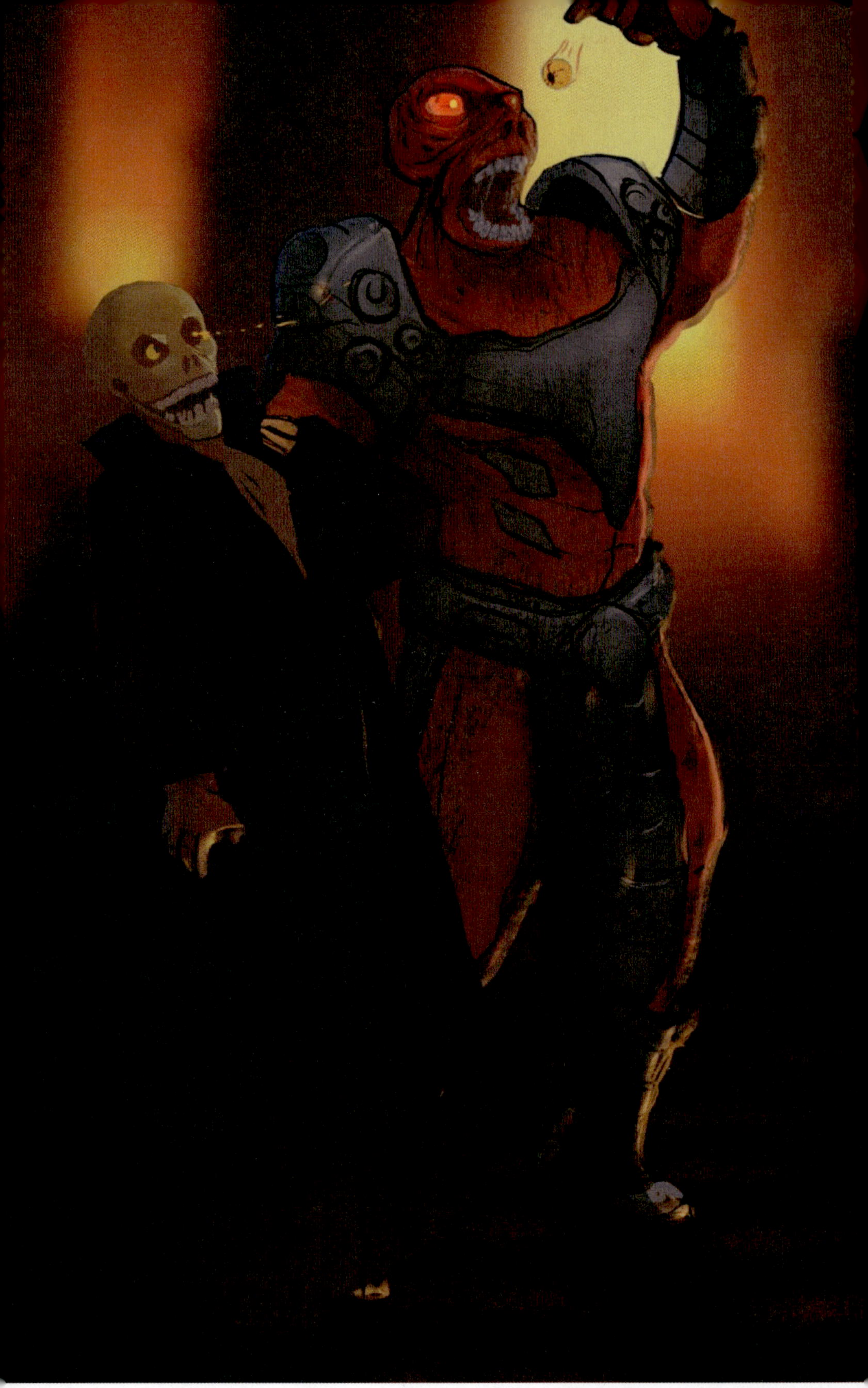

UNKNOWN VS SATAN

In a final act of triumph, UNKNOWN THE SLASHER rips off Satan's head with mighty claws, displaying it like a trophy on a stick near the throne. In this victorious moment, UNKNOWN THE SLASHER seizes control of hell's realm, ending Satan's reign of terror.

Acknowledged for his valor and triumph, UNKNOWN THE SLASHER is bestowed a crown by a celestial angel. This crown symbolizes his newfound authority and strength, empowering him to confront even greater challenges ahead. With his victory over Satan, UNKNOWN THE SLASHER's reputation as the champion of two worlds — hell and earth — is solidified.

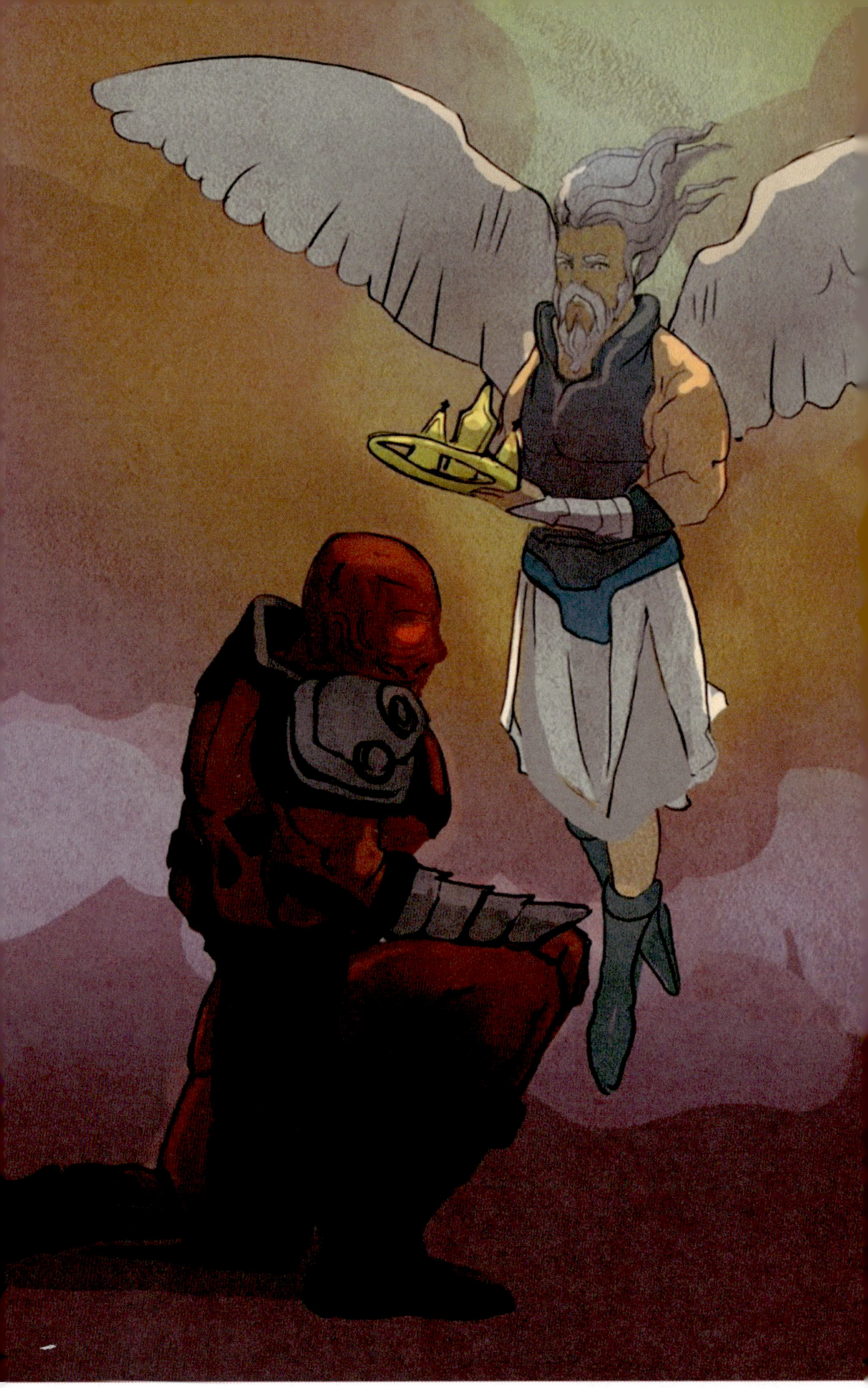

UNKNOWN VS SATAN

The ground trembles beneath UNKNOWN's feet, a testament to the seismic shift in power. His upgraded crown signifies his unrivaled status as the conqueror of all evil, honored by divine recognition from God and Jesus Christ. UNKNOWN THE SLASHER's conquest stands as a pivotal moment in history, marking the defeat of evil's darkest forces and ushering in a new era of hope and righteousness.

After gaining control of Satan's powers, UNKNOWN THE SLASHER wielded immense authority over all evil acts throughout history, spanning centuries of battles dating back to ancient Rome. His mission remained steadfast: to protect the innocent from the grips of malevolence.

One notable figure from history was a black slave owner who, despite being enslaved himself, inflicted unimaginable suffering upon others. UNKNOWN THE SLASHER intervened, summoning demons to capture the man and condemn him to hell's prison. There, he endured a relentless punishment — engulfed in lightning bolts of electricity, a torment no mortal could endure.

Across the world, daily trials tested humanity, each a testament to divine providence. UNKNOWN THE SLASHER navigated through these challenges, using his newfound powers to confront evil head-on. As he ascended through the elevator, now bearing his name instead of Satan's, he encountered a scene in Jamaica: a chaotic street brawl involving a woman.

Amidst the chaos, this woman caught UNKNOWN THE

SLASHER's attention not with fear or violence, but with an act of love. It was in this moment that God, represented by Jesus Christ, appeared to commend UNKNOWN THE SLASHER for his tireless efforts in combating the torment inflicted by Satan upon humanity. Yet, even amidst these victories, UNKNOWN THE SLASHER knew his duty was far from over.

Acknowledging the praise from Jesus, UNKNOWN THE SLASHER remained resolute in his commitment to eradicate evil from the world. Though his path was fraught with darkness, Jesus reassured him of a place in heaven, where many rooms awaited those who believed in God's promise. With gratitude and determination, UNKNOWN THE SLASHER accepted his role as the champion of hell's realm, unwavering in his quest to bring justice and peace to a world besieged by malevolence.

In these moments of reflection and divine affirmation, UNKNOWN THE SLASHER found solace in knowing that his actions, however harsh, were guided by a higher purpose — to cleanse the world of evil and ensure that goodness prevailed.

The Lord's Prayer

The Lord's Prayer, found in Matthew 6:9-13, outlines a sacred invocation taught by Jesus to his disciples. It begins with reverence: "Our Father in heaven, hallowed be your name," acknowledging God's holiness and sovereignty over all creation. The prayer continues with a plea for God's kingdom to come and His will to be done on earth as it is in heaven, affirming the desire for divine order and righteousness to prevail universally. It includes petitions for daily sustenance ("Give us today our daily bread") and forgiveness of sins ("And forgive us our debts, as we also have forgiven our debtors"). There is also a supplication for divine guidance and protection: "And lead us not into temptation, but deliver us from the evil one."

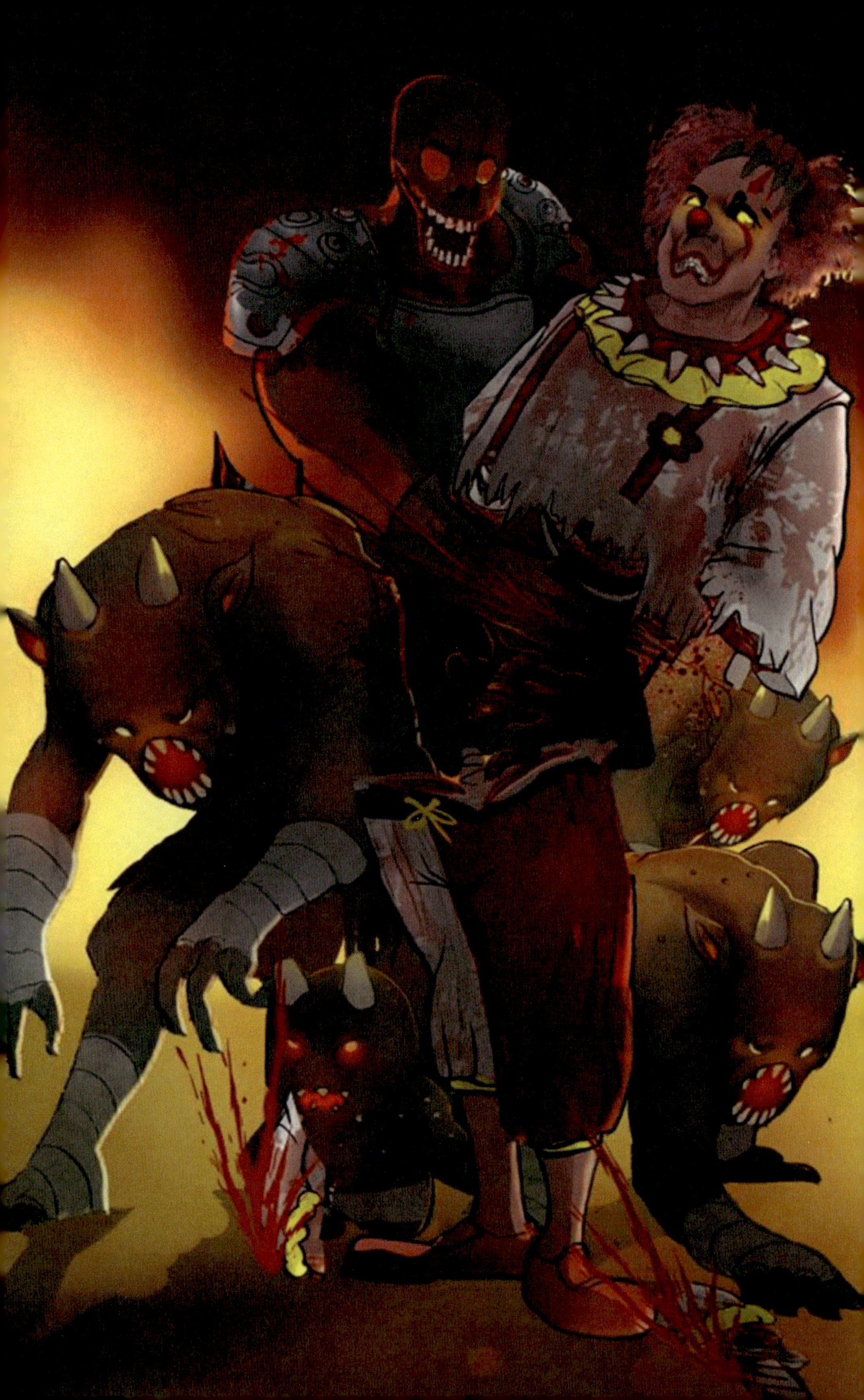

UNKNOWN VS SATAN

In UNKNOWN THE SLASHER's realm, a significant transformation occurs as crime rates plummet under his rule of hell. However, a lingering threat persists in the form of a malevolent clown and his three demonic cohorts wreaking havoc in small cities. UNKNOWN THE SLASHER, after a necessary week of rest to regain strength, takes up the mantle to restore peace and ensure a world free from criminality for generations to come.

The battle is fierce as UNKNOWN THE SLASHER confronts the clown and his minions. With determination and skill, UNKNOWN THE SLASHER swiftly dispatches the clown, severing him in a single decisive blow that spills blood through the streets. The three demons, once under the clown's control, falter in shock and fear, disintegrating as their leader falls.

Amidst the turmoil, a divine presence shines through. The heavens, illuminated by the glory of God and the Lord Jesus Christ, radiate a serene blue brilliance that reflects the beauty and grace of the Almighty. UNKNOWN THE SLASHER, humbled by this sight, offers reverence and love to God, acknowledging His greatness and seeking forgiveness for any transgressions committed in the pursuit of justice.

Luke 11:21-28 presents a powerful metaphor about spiritual warfare and the triumph of good over evil. It illustrates how a strong man, well-armed and vigilant, protects his house, ensuring safety and security for all within. Yet, when a stronger adversary arrives and defeats him, this invader seizes control, disarming the former defender and reshaping the fate of those within his domain.

BRADLEY T. LIVINGSTON

In UNKNOWN THE SLASHER's journey, haunted by childhood nightmares of demonic encounters orchestrated by Satan's minions, a profound realization dawns upon him. He must confront and defeat these demonic forces, starting with Muzan, the formidable King of Demons, to assert dominion over both realms of evil.

SATAN

MUZAN

To access Muzan's dark domain, UNKNOWN THE SLASHER embarks on a perilous quest to Russia's hellish side. There, he seeks the Black Tourmaline Crystal, a key artifact required to unlock the hidden button in the hell's elevator. This crystal, once inserted into the panel beside UNKNOWN THE SLASHER's compartment, reveals the elusive black button that grants passage to the depths below hell's realm—an abyss cloaked in impenetrable darkness, untouched by any semblance of light.

With determination and resolve, UNKNOWN THE SLASHER presses forward into this eerie, spectral realm, prepared to face Muzan in an ultimate battle of fate and destiny. In a vast arena shrouded in black clouds and swirling mists, the demon lord awaits, poised for conflict. UNKNOWN THE SLASHER confronts Muzan with righteous anger, accusing him of tormenting humanity through his malevolent armies.

The clash is fierce and relentless. UNKNOWN THE SLASHER's claws, honed to razor-sharp perfection, tear through the darkness, striking at Muzan's heart with unyielding force. As the battle reaches its climax, the ground trembles beneath their feet, resonating with the monumental struggle unfolding between them.

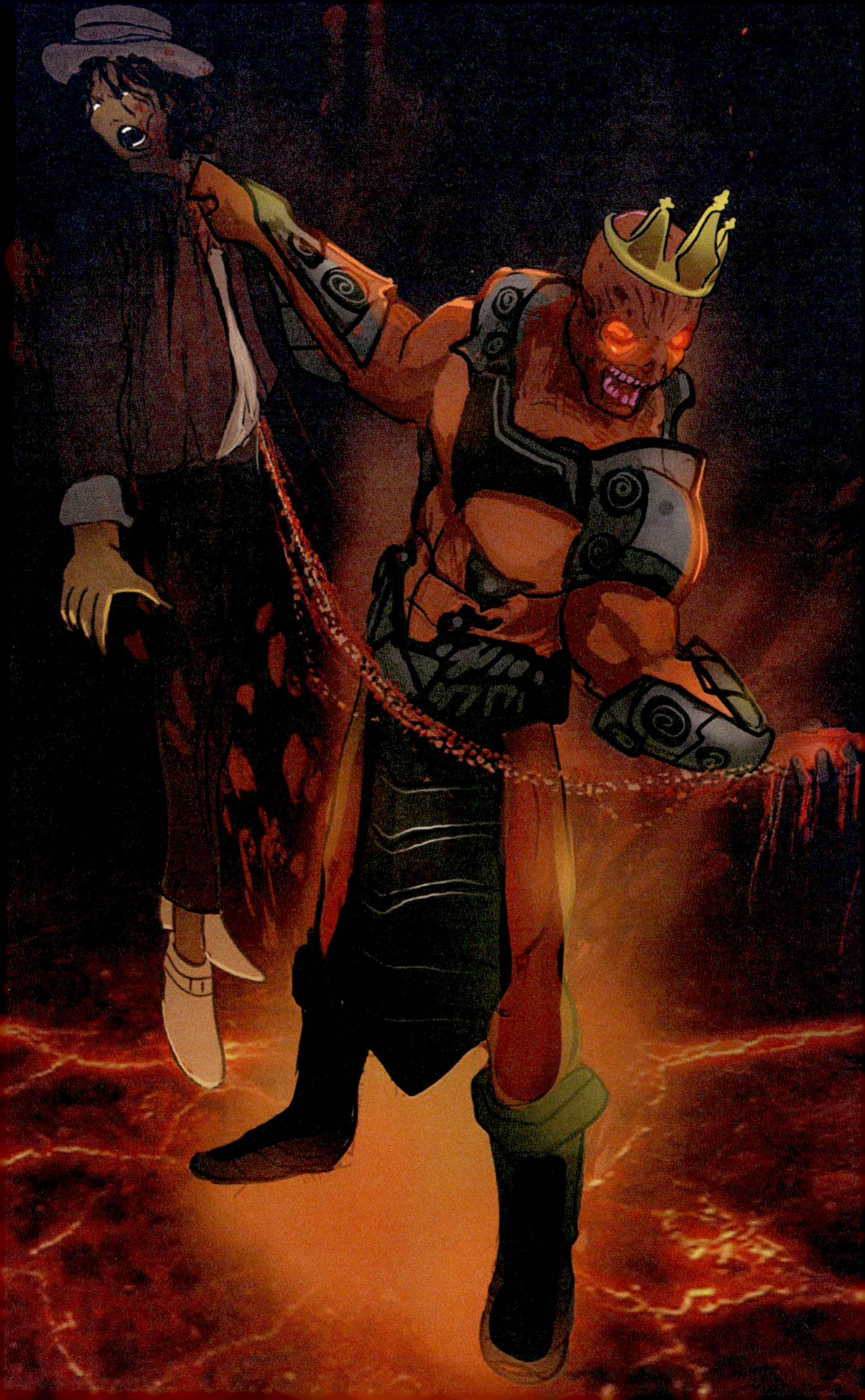

In the aftermath of this cataclysmic duel, UNKNOWN THE SLASHER emerges victorious. His crown, symbolizing unparalleled authority over all realms of evil, gleams with newfound power and glory. It signifies his triumph over Muzan and his dominion over the twin worlds of malevolence—a testament to the divine favor bestowed upon him by God and the Lord Jesus Christ.

Luke 11:21-28's analogy resonates deeply in UNKNOWN THE SLASHER's conquest. It underscores the principle that spiritual strength and determination are necessary to overcome darkness and uphold righteousness. By aligning himself with the divine will and confronting evil head-on, UNKNOWN THE SLASHER fulfills his destiny as the champion against all forms of wickedness, ensuring that evil's grip on humanity is shattered from top to bottom.

In reflection, UNKNOWN THE SLASHER acknowledges the profound guidance and support of God and the Lord Jesus Christ throughout his journey. He understands that his path, though fraught with trials and temptations, is illuminated by the promise of eternal victory and salvation. As he continues to wield his newfound authority with humility and purpose, UNKNOWN THE SLASHER remains steadfast in his commitment to righteousness, guided by the timeless wisdom of Luke 11:21-28 and the enduring love of his divine benefactors.

In the aftermath of the city's devastation, UNKNOWN THE SLASHER found himself amidst scenes of chaos and despair. Streets once bustling with life were now reduced to rubble and debris, with shattered buildings and plumes of smoke filling the air. The destruction weighed heavily on UNKNOWN THE SLASHER's heart as he witnessed the aftermath of such relentless cruelty. The loss of innocent lives and the ruin of homes and livelihoods served as a stark reminder of the forces they were up against.

However, amidst the devastation, signs of resilience and hope emerged. Survivors, determined and steadfast, began the daunting task of rebuilding their shattered community. UNKNOWN THE SLASHER wasted no time in joining their efforts, lending a helping hand to clear debris and provide assistance wherever possible. Together, they worked tirelessly, driven by a shared determination to reclaim their city from darkness.

As UNKNOWN THE SLASHER navigated through the rubble, he encountered a diverse array of people—men, women, and children—who had united in defiance against the malevolent forces that had wrought such destruction. They looked to him with admiration and gratitude, seeing in him a symbol of hope amidst the devastation. Despite the challenges ahead, UNKNOWN THE SLASHER remained resolute in his belief that together they could overcome adversity.

Yet, even as they labored to rebuild, reports arrived of similar attacks unfolding in neighboring cities. It became clear that this was not an isolated incident but part of a coordinated campaign by a dark force intent on spreading chaos and fear. Determined to confront this threat, UNKNOWN THE SLASHER embarked on a journey to rally support and forge alliances.

BRADLEY T. LIVINGSTON

During his travels, UNKNOWN THE SLASHER encountered remarkable individuals—legends of combat, wise scholars, and skilled healers—all of whom possessed unique abilities crucial to their cause. Alongside them, he met ordinary people whose resilience and newfound strength became pillars of their resistance.

Together, they formed a diverse coalition united by a common purpose: to protect the innocent and combat the forces of darkness. They trained rigorously, honing their skills and devising strategies to anticipate and counter their adversaries' moves.

Despite their preparations, an undercurrent of foreboding lingered. UNKNOWN THE SLASHER knew their enemy was cunning and relentless, and the impending conflict would test their resolve like never before. As the days passed, tension mounted, and UNKNOWN THE SLASHER and his allies prepared themselves mentally and physically for the inevitable confrontation.

They understood the stakes were high—the fate of their world hung in the balance. Only through unity and unwavering determination could they hope to emerge victorious against an enemy bent on destruction.

In the face of uncertainty, UNKNOWN THE SLASHER and his allies stood firm, drawing strength from their collective resolve and the support of those they had rallied to their cause. Together, they faced the challenge before them, ready to confront the darkness and restore hope to a world in need of healing and renewal.

As the days stretched into weeks, UNKNOWN THE

SLASHER and his coalition of allies remained steadfast in their preparations for the imminent battle. They dedicated themselves to rigorous training, sharpening their combat skills and refining their strategies. Each member brought unique strengths to the team, creating a formidable force against the encroaching darkness. Amidst their intense preparations, UNKNOWN THE SLASHER sought wisdom from the venerable elders of the land. These wise figures possessed ancient knowledge passed down through generations, offering insights crucial to understanding their formidable enemy.

Through the elders' guidance, UNKNOWN THE SLASHER learned of the origins of the malevolent force they faced. It was a creature of immense power, born from the deepest abyss of the underworld and fueled by centuries of hatred and malice. Its sole purpose was the annihilation of all that was good and pure, relentless in its pursuit of sinister goals. Armed with this knowledge, UNKNOWN THE SLASHER and his allies devised a daring plan to confront their adversary head-on. They knew the impending battle would be fraught with peril, yet they were resolved to face it with unwavering courage.

As the day of reckoning approached, tension mounted within the coalition. Fear and uncertainty loomed, but they drew strength from their unity, knowing they fought not only for their survival but for the future of their world. Finally, the fateful day arrived. UNKNOWN THE SLASHER and his allies assembled at the city's edge, steeling themselves for the confrontation ahead. Anticipation crackled in the air as they readied to march into the heart of darkness and confront their nemesis.

With a resounding battle cry, they surged forward, weapons gleaming in the sunlight as they clashed with the forces of evil. The conflict erupted into a fierce struggle, each side unleashing their most potent attacks in a desperate bid for supremacy. UNKNOWN THE SLASHER led the charge, his claws slashing through enemy ranks as he sought the heart of their opposition. With each strike, he drew nearer to the epicenter of darkness, determined to deliver the decisive blow that would end the chaos once and for all.

Yet, amidst the tumult of battle, UNKNOWN THE SLASHER sensed a troubling realization taking shape. Their enemy seemed to anticipate their every move, countering with uncanny precision. It was as if an unseen hand guided their foes, exploiting vulnerabilities with devastating effectiveness. As UNKNOWN THE SLASHER grappled with this revelation, a swift movement caught his eye amidst the chaos—a figure lurking in the shadows, observing the conflict with a malevolent intent.

Recognition dawned on UNKNOWN THE SLASHER as he identified the figure for what it truly was—the mastermind behind their enemy's machinations, orchestrating events from the shadows to further its dark agenda. With renewed determination, UNKNOWN THE SLASHER rallied his allies, directing their focus towards the lurking figure. Together, they launched a relentless assault, driving the sinister entity back until it was forced to reveal itself in its entirety.

As the truth came to light, UNKNOWN THE SLASHER felt

a surge of adrenaline. With a mighty roar, he hurled himself at the malevolent figure, claws extended and poised for the final strike. The battle reached its climax as UNKNOWN THE SLASHER's blows landed true, each strike fueled by the collective resolve of his allies. With a decisive thrust, he pierced through the darkness, bringing an end to the malevolent force's grip on their world.

Victory was theirs, but the cost had been high. Amidst the aftermath, UNKNOWN THE SLASHER stood amidst the debris, reflecting on the trials endured and the sacrifices made. The path ahead remained uncertain, yet they had prevailed against overwhelming odds. UNKNOWN THE SLASHER looked to his comrades, a silent acknowledgment passing between them—a testament to their resilience and the bond forged through adversity.

As they began the task of rebuilding, UNKNOWN THE SLASHER knew that their journey was far from over. They had faced darkness head-on and emerged victorious, but the echoes of their battle would resonate throughout the ages—a testament to their courage and the enduring strength of the human spirit against the forces of evil.

As UNKNOWN THE SLASHER and his allies pressed forward, determined to track down their elusive adversary, the landscape around them underwent a transformation. Leaving behind the wreckage of the city, they ventured into dense forests that gradually gave way to rolling hills adorned with lush greenery and vibrant wildflowers. The air carried the sweet fragrance of blossoms, and the songs of birds filled the valleys, creating a contrast to the chaos they had left behind.

Despite the serene surroundings, an undercurrent of unease persisted. UNKNOWN THE SLASHER remained vigilant, acutely aware of the lurking danger. He knew their enemies could strike at any moment, prompting him to scan the horizon with heightened senses. As they journeyed onward, they encountered a tranquil village nestled at the base of the hills—a haven untouched by the devastation that had befallen other parts of the land.

The villagers welcomed UNKNOWN THE SLASHER and his allies warmly, offering them food and shelter for the night. Grateful for the respite, they gratefully accepted the hospitality, finding refuge within the safety of the village walls. Around the crackling fire that evening, the villagers shared tales of their homeland and the hardships they faced in the aftermath of enemy attacks. They spoke of lost loved ones, homes reduced to rubble, and dreams shattered by the relentless advance of darkness.

Listening intently, UNKNOWN THE SLASHER's heart weighed heavy with empathy for the villagers' plight. He understood their suffering as a microcosm of the larger tragedy unfolding across the land. Their stories reinforced his resolve to continue the quest despite the challenges ahead.

As night descended, UNKNOWN THE SLASHER and his allies settled into makeshift beds, their minds swirling with thoughts of the trials awaiting them. The following morning, they bid farewell to their gracious hosts, knowing their journey would lead them deeper into perilous territory. With each step, they ascended into the rugged hills, the path growing steeper as they approached towering peaks cloaked in mist.

The air thinned and the temperature dropped, signaling their ascent into the unforgiving heights of the mountains. Yet, undeterred by the harsh conditions, UNKNOWN THE SLASHER and his companions pressed onward. Their determination was unwavering, bolstered by the knowledge that their enemies lurked in the shadows, plotting their next move.

As they traversed the treacherous terrain, UNKNOWN THE SLASHER remained alert, his senses attuned to signs of danger. He knew they were drawing closer to their elusive foe, the malevolent force that had orchestrated so much destruction. Each passing hour brought them nearer to the heart of darkness they sought to vanquish.

Despite the physical and emotional toll of their journey, UNKNOWN THE SLASHER found strength in the unity of his allies. They moved with purpose, united in their quest to confront evil and restore peace to their world. Along the way, they encountered challenges that tested their resolve—natural obstacles, fatigue, and the constant threat of ambush. Yet through it all, they persevered, drawing courage from their shared commitment to justice and the protection of innocent lives.

As they neared their destination, UNKNOWN THE SLASHER's anticipation grew. He knew that the final confrontation with their adversary loomed ahead—a battle that would require every ounce of their skill and determination. But he also knew they were prepared, strengthened by their journey and fortified by the bonds forged in adversity.

With the towering peaks of the mountains looming overhead, UNKNOWN THE SLASHER and his allies stood ready to face whatever lay ahead. Their eyes were fixed on the horizon, unwavering in their resolve to confront the darkness and emerge victorious. The echoes of their footsteps reverberated through the mountains, a testament to their courage as they pressed forward into the unknown, guided by hope and fueled by the belief that good would prevail over evil.

As they ascended to the summit of the tallest peak, the terrain grew increasingly desolate, the once-lush vegetation giving way to rocky outcrops and barren cliffs. The arduous journey had tested their endurance, but finally, they stood at the pinnacle, catching their breath amidst a panoramic view of their devastated homeland. Below them sprawled the ruins of once-great cities, now reduced to smoldering rubble, and once-fertile fields lay barren and lifeless.

Amidst the desolation, however, there were flickers of hope—small signs of life that renewed their resolve. A wise old sage they encountered informed them that their enemy's stronghold lay across the valley. Armed with this knowledge, UNKNOWN THE SLASHER and his allies prepared to descend from the mountain. They knew the path ahead would be perilous, yet they drew strength from their unity and determination to confront evil together.

UNKNOWN VS SATAN

Descending from the rugged peaks, anticipation filled the air. The landscape unfolded in breathtaking vistas—rolling hills cascading into verdant valleys, where clear streams wound through lush undergrowth. Towering trees cast dappled shadows, their leaves rustling in the breeze.

Beneath this serene surface, however, danger lurked. Jagged rocks and deep ravines posed threats, while unseen predators stalked within dense foliage. Despite these challenges, UNKNOWN THE SLASHER and his companions pressed onward with unwavering courage. Each step brought them deeper into the wilderness, their senses alert to the nuances of the untamed environment.

Navigating the treacherous terrain demanded vigilance. They crossed rushing rivers, navigated narrow mountain passes, and scaled sheer cliffs. Progress was deliberate, each movement calculated to avoid pitfalls. As they ventured further, signs of their adversaries emerged—footprints marking paths, ancient symbols on stones, and eerie whispers echoing through the forest.

The realization that they were not alone heightened their awareness. UNKNOWN THE SLASHER and his allies maintained readiness, weapons poised and minds sharp. They encountered challenges that tested their skills—a sudden ambush by lurking foes, treacherous terrain that demanded careful navigation, and the constant threat of ambush.

Through perseverance and unity, they forged ahead. Their journey became a testament to resilience and determination in the face of adversity. They adapted to the wilderness, learning its rhythms and respecting its dangers. Each encounter with danger strengthened their bond, reinforcing their shared purpose.

As they delved deeper, the landscape grew more forbidding. The wilderness revealed its secrets—a hidden cave concealing ancient artifacts, a forgotten altar inscribed with cryptic runes, and the remnants of a campfire suggesting recent activity. Each discovery fueled their determination to press forward, to uncover the truth behind their enemy's plans.

Days turned into weeks as they navigated the wilds. UNKNOWN THE SLASHER's leadership guided them through trials and tribulations. They faced setbacks—a sudden storm that forced them to seek shelter, an injured comrade requiring urgent care—but they persisted, driven by a shared vision of justice and peace.

Their resolve never wavered, even as the challenges mounted. They encountered tests of strength and cunning—a narrow escape from a collapsing bridge, a tense negotiation with wary locals, and a strategic ambush that tested their combat skills. Through it all, UNKNOWN THE SLASHER's wisdom and resolve inspired his allies, rallying them in moments of doubt.

As they approached the enemy stronghold, tension crackled in the air. UNKNOWN THE SLASHER and his companions prepared for the final confrontation—a battle that would determine the fate of their world. They steeled themselves for what lay ahead, their hearts heavy with the weight of responsibility yet fortified by their unwavering courage.

With each step closer to their adversary's lair, UNKNOWN THE SLASHER's determination burned brighter. He knew that the time had come to confront the darkness that threatened their homeland. His allies stood beside him, united in purpose and ready to face whatever challenges awaited them. Together, they marched onward, their hearts set on victory and their spirits undaunted by the perils that lay ahead.

As UNKNOWN THE SLASHER and his companions ventured deeper into their journey, they drew strength from their unwavering bond and shared purpose. Each obstacle they faced—from battling fierce beasts to navigating treacherous terrain—only solidified their resolve. Together, they formed a powerful alliance, determined to rid their world of evil and restore peace.

Their path was fraught with challenges and hardships. They endured storms and hardships with courage, their spirits undaunted. Through it all, they remained steadfast in their commitment to their mission.

As they traveled onward, UNKNOWN THE SLASHER and his companions knew the road ahead would be difficult. Yet, with their hearts set on their goal and their eyes fixed on the horizon, they pressed forward. They were ready to confront whatever challenges lay ahead, driven by their pursuit of justice and redemption.

As dusk fell and the sky painted itself in fiery hues, UNKNOWN THE SLASHER and his companions made camp for the night. Around a crackling fire, they sought warmth and solace from the mountain's cold embrace. Shadows flickered, casting dancing shapes on tired faces.

The day had been taxing, filled with peril and hardship. They had scaled cliffs, battled beasts, and navigated treacherous terrain. Despite the dangers, they persevered, fueled by their shared purpose. In the quiet of the night, their thoughts turned to the daunting task ahead—confronting their enemy to end the chaos gripping their homeland. They knew the journey would test them, but failure was not an option. The fate of their world depended on their courage.

Through the night, UNKNOWN THE SLASHER and his companions kept watch, alert to the forest's mysteries. Ancient trees whispered in the wind, and unknown creatures prowled nearby. Despite the eerie atmosphere, their determination remained unshaken. They understood the stakes—they had to face their fears head-on to succeed.

With dawn, they resumed their journey through the dense forest. Its labyrinthine paths and dense foliage threatened to ensnare them, but they pressed on. Their spirits lifted by camaraderie and shared purpose, they knew they weren't alone in their quest.

Every step brought them closer to their enemy's stronghold. UNKNOWN THE SLASHER's leadership guided them through challenges, each one a test of their resolve. They braved dangers—a sudden storm, a fallen comrade's injury—but they persisted. Their journey became a testament to courage and determination in the face

As they battled their way through the stronghold, the oppressive dark magic grew stronger, distorting the very air around them. The enemy's sorcerers unleashed torrents of arcane energy, their spells crackling with malevolent power. Yet, UNKNOWN THE SLASHER and his allies pressed onward, their determination unwavering despite the overwhelming odds against them.

After a relentless push, they finally breached the inner sanctum of the stronghold where the source of the dark magic awaited them. A towering figure, shrouded in shadow, confronted them with eyes glowing ominously. Its voice carried the weight of ancient power as it spoke disdainfully.

"You dare challenge me? Foolish mortals, you will know true despair."

In response, UNKNOWN THE SLASHER stepped forward, clutching the Key of Aether which emitted a brilliant glow. "Your reign of terror ends here."

Activating the talisman with a surge of power, its radiant light pierced through the darkness, dispelling the stronghold's protective enchantments. The figure recoiled, its form flickering as the malevolent magic was stripped away.

With a resounding battle cry, UNKNOWN THE SLASHER and his companions launched their final assault. Their combined strength overwhelmed the enemy in a fierce battle, each blow resonating with their unyielding resolve. Ultimately, it was UNKNOWN THE SLASHER who delivered the decisive strike, his companions drew nearer to their destination—the enemy stronghold looming across the valley. Each step brought them closer to the final confrontation, filling their hearts with a mix of apprehension and anticipation. They understood the magnitude of the battle ahead, knowing their courage and resolve would face their ultimate test. Pressing onward into uncertainty, they carried the hopes and aspirations of their people. They weren't merely warriors seeking vengeance; they embodied justice and defenders of the innocent. With their sights set on their shared objective and their spirits unyielding to the trials ahead, they advanced resolutely, prepared for whatever obstacles lay in their path to triumph.

The journey to the enemy stronghold tested UNKNOWN THE SLASHER and his companions to their limits. Venturing deeper into the valley, the terrain grew increasingly perilous, the atmosphere heavy with foreboding. Each stride felt like a battle against an unseen malevolence permeating the wilderness.

One morning, as dawn broke through the dense canopy, UNKNOWN THE SLASHER and his allies approached a narrow gorge. Spanning the chasm was a precarious bridge swaying above a seemingly bottomless abyss. Emerging from the shadows, a group of fellow travelers greeted them—a diverse assembly of warriors, mages, and scouts united by a shared purpose.

"We've been observing your journey," remarked Kalen, a weathered warrior among them. "Your determination is commendable, but the path ahead holds dangers unlike any you've faced. The stronghold is heavily fortified, and the enemy anticipates an attack."

UNKNOWN THE SLASHER nodded solemnly, his gaze unwavering. "Turning back is not an option now. Whatever challenges await us, we will confront them, no matter the cost."

Kalen's expression softened into a grim smile. "Then let us combine our strengths. Together, our chances of overcoming the enemy are greater."

With a shared understanding of the perilous task ahead, UNKNOWN THE SLASHER and his newfound allies forged an alliance. They strategized, pooling their skills and knowledge, preparing for the decisive battle that would determine the fate of their world. Each member brought unique abilities to the table, their unity a beacon of hope amidst the encroaching darkness.

As they readied themselves for the final push towards the enemy stronghold, a sense of camaraderie and determination filled the air. They knew the odds were against them, yet their resolve burned brighter than ever. Their journey had led them to this pivotal moment—to stand together against evil, to fight for justice, and to protect all they held dear.

With every step, UNKNOWN THE SLASHER and his allies moved closer to their ultimate confrontation. The weight of responsibility rested heavy on their shoulders, but they drew strength from each other. They were ready to face whatever awaited them on the battlefield, driven by a shared purpose that transcended individual fears and uncertainties.

Together, they marched forward into the unknown, their hearts unified in a resolute pursuit of victory against the forces of darkness that threatened to engulf their world.

With their numbers bolstered by the arrival of new allies, the combined group cautiously traversed the swaying bridge, each step a testament to their bravery. On the opposite side, the forest yielded to jagged cliffs and rocky formations, creating a complex maze that obscured their path to the enemy stronghold. The air carried the earthy scent of moss and the distant rumble of waterfalls, adding urgency to their journey.

Navigating the perilous terrain, they encountered traps and ambushes laid by the enemy's scouts. Hidden pitfalls and triggered snares slowed their progress, necessitating careful, deliberate movement. Leading the way, UNKNOWN THE SLASHER remained vigilant, his senses attuned to every potential danger. As they overcame each obstacle, their camaraderie deepened, becoming a beacon of hope amid encroaching shadows.

One evening, as they set camp in a sheltered alcove, a solitary figure approached draped in a weathered cloak. The figure lowered their hood, revealing the wise face of an elderly sage.

"I am Elyria," she spoke softly, her voice carrying through the night. "I have watched your journey and bring a warning. The stronghold is shielded by potent magic—a dark sorcery that distorts reality. To defeat the enemy, you must first dispel this enchantment."

UNKNOWN THE SLASHER focused intently, his gaze

narrowing. "How can we break this enchantment?"

Elyria produced a small, intricately carved talisman. "This is the Key of Aether. It can dispel the dark magic surrounding the stronghold, but it must be activated within the heart of the enemy's domain. Beware, for the enemy will resist with all their might."

Armed with the talisman, UNKNOWN THE SLASHER and his comrades resumed their march, their determination unwavering. The journey to the stronghold was fraught with peril, each step forward a battle against malevolent forces. They faced relentless assaults from shadowy creatures and spectral wraiths, their resolve tested by the essence of pure evil.

At long last, they emerged from the labyrinthine cliffs to confront the enemy stronghold. It loomed like an ominous sentinel, its towering walls and spiked defenses enveloped in a swirling vortex of dark energy. The air buzzed with palpable tension, the ground trembling beneath their feet from the fortress's overwhelming power.

UNKNOWN THE SLASHER turned to his companions, his voice steady. "This is our moment. The battle awaits. Together, we will confront the enemy and bring an end to this darkness."

With a resounding battle cry, the group surged forward toward the stronghold, weapons raised and hearts braced for the impending fight. The ground shook as they clashed with the enemy's forces, the clash of steel and magic reverberating across the valley. Leading the charge, UNKNOWN THE SLASHER's blade moved swiftly, cutting through the ranks of dark warriors blocking their path.

As they battled their way through the stronghold, the oppressive dark magic grew stronger, distorting the very air around them. The enemy's sorcerers unleashed torrents of arcane energy, their spells crackling with malevolent power. Yet, UNKNOWN THE SLASHER and his allies pressed onward, their determination unwavering despite the overwhelming odds against them.

After a relentless push, they finally breached the inner sanctum of the stronghold where the source of the dark magic awaited them. A towering figure, shrouded in shadow, confronted them with eyes glowing ominously. Its voice carried the weight of ancient power as it spoke disdainfully.

"You dare challenge me? Foolish mortals, you will know true despair."

In response, UNKNOWN THE SLASHER stepped forward, clutching the Key of Aether which emitted a brilliant glow. "Your reign of terror ends here."

Activating the talisman with a surge of power, its radiant light pierced through the darkness, dispelling the stronghold's protective enchantments. The figure recoiled, its form flickering as the malevolent magic was stripped away.

With a resounding battle cry, UNKNOWN THE SLASHER and his companions launched their final assault. Their combined strength overwhelmed the enemy in a fierce battle, each blow resonating with their unyielding resolve. Ultimately, it was UNKNOWN THE SLASHER who delivered the decisive strike, his blade cutting through the darkness to vanquish the enemy once and for all.

As the remnants of dark magic dispersed, the stronghold crumbled, leaving the valley bathed in the light of dawn. UNKNOWN THE SLASHER and his companions stood victorious, their hearts swelling with the knowledge that they had triumphed over evil.

Together, they had faced adversity head-on and emerged victorious, their courage and determination serving as a beacon of hope for those who would follow in their footsteps. Standing amidst the ruins, they savored a brief moment of respite, basking in the hard-earned peace that had eluded them for so long.

However, the initial euphoria of victory soon gave way to a sobering realization. While they had won the battle, the war was far from over. The land bore scars from the enemy's devastation, and the daunting task of rebuilding lay ahead. UNKNOWN THE SLASHER understood that their journey was far from complete.

"We did it," Kalen murmured, his voice tinged with relief and exhaustion. "But what comes next?"

UNKNOWN THE SLASHER surveyed his comrades, their faces reflecting a mix of determination and weariness. "Now, we begin the next phase of our journey. We must help our people rebuild and ensure that such darkness never threatens our land again."

With that solemn commitment, UNKNOWN THE SLASHER and his companions prepared to embark on the challenging path of recovery and restoration. They knew that rebuilding their homeland would require resilience, unity, and unwavering dedication. But they also knew that as long as they stood together, they could face any challenge that lay ahead, ensuring a brighter future for all.

As the group embarked on the monumental task of clearing rubble and caring for the wounded, they discovered survivors among the debris—men, women, and children who had hidden or been imprisoned during the enemy's reign. Initially fearful, their faces soon brightened with hope as they realized the nightmare was finally over. Days turned into weeks as UNKNOWN THE SLASHER and his allies, alongside the survivors, worked tirelessly to transform the stronghold from a symbol of oppression into a beacon of resilience. Bonds strengthened as they labored together in rebuilding their shattered land.

One evening, bathed in the warm glow of the setting sun over their bustling camp, Elyria approached UNKNOWN THE SLASHER. Her eyes, filled with both wisdom and sorrow, carried the weight of centuries as she spoke softly.

"You have done admirably," she began, her voice solemn. "But there is something you must understand. The dark force we defeated here was just a fragment of a greater evil. Others like it lurk across the land, waiting to rise."

UNKNOWN THE SLASHER's heart sank at her words, but his determination only grew stronger. "Then we will find them and eliminate them. We cannot let this darkness spread." Elyria nodded knowingly. "Your bravery is commendable, but remember the importance of balance. The land is wounded, and its healing will require both strength and wisdom."

Reflecting on her words, UNKNOWN THE SLASHER realized their truth. The battles had not only scarred the land but also tested their spirits. They needed to rebuild not only homes and fields but also the resilience and unity of their people.

Armed with this realization, UNKNOWN THE SLASHER gathered his companions and shared Elyria's warning. Together, they pledged to seek out and destroy the remaining pockets of darkness while nurturing the newfound hope in their hearts. Their journey continued, now focused on healing and growth.

In the days that followed, they encountered challenges and moments of hope. UNKNOWN THE SLASHER and his allies traveled from village to village, offering aid wherever it was needed. They defended against occasional remnants of dark forces but more often found themselves helping to reconstruct homes, sow fields, and impart lessons of unity and strength to the next generation.

In one village, they met Mira, a young girl who had lost her family to the darkness. UNKNOWN THE SLASHER took her under his wing, teaching her the ways of a warrior while also emphasizing compassion and kindness. Mira's spirit remained unbroken, becoming a symbol of resilience and hope for the villagers.

As they journeyed onward, UNKNOWN THE SLASHER took time to contemplate his own path. He sought wisdom from elders and sages, learning from their experiences and gaining a deeper understanding of the delicate balance between light and darkness. He realized that true strength derived not solely from wielding a blade but from the harmonious union of heart and mind. One day, while passing through a dense forest, they stumbled upon an ancient temple obscured by vines and moss. Inside, a library awaited them, filled with scrolls and tomes chronicling the land's history and the age-old struggles between light and shadow. UNKNOWN THE SLASHER immersed himself in these texts, seeking insights that could aid them in their ongoing quest.

Among the scrolls, he uncovered references to an ancient artifact known as the Heart of Aether—a potent relic reputed to possess the ability to cleanse even the deepest darkness. Legend spoke of its concealment by a forgotten order of guardians, its whereabouts entrusted to a select few.

Armed with this newfound knowledge, UNKNOWN THE SLASHER understood that their journey had taken on a profound new dimension. The Heart of Aether held promise not only for vanquishing the lingering remnants of darkness but also for restoring harmony to the ravaged land.

Gathering his companions, UNKNOWN THE SLASHER shared his discovery. Their eyes gleamed with resolve and optimism. "We must locate the Heart of Aether," he proclaimed. "It could be the pivotal factor in bringing an end to this conflict once and for all."

Thus, with a clear objective before them, UNKNOWN THE SLASHER and his comrades embarked on the next chapter of their odyssey. Their quest for the Heart of Aether would lead them through uncharted territories, unveiling new challenges and unearthing ancient secrets along the way. The path ahead brimmed with peril, yet buoyed by shared purpose and unyielding determination, they believed themselves capable of surmounting any obstacle. Together, they remained steadfast in their commitment to uphold justice and foster peace, their resolve unwavering even in the face of adversity.

As they pressed forward, they carried not only their own aspirations but also the collective hopes and aspirations of their people. UNITED THE SLASHER knew they were destined to forge a brighter future for all who called the land their home, driven by their unwavering dedication to safeguarding the light against encroaching darkness.

As UNKNOWN THE SLASHER and his companions ventured forth in their quest for the Heart of Aether, they traversed lands rich with tales of heroism and ancient struggles. Every village they visited, every ruin they explored, whispered stories of valor and conflict that spanned generations. These narratives served as both inspiration and cautionary tales, reminding them of the perpetual battle between light and darkness, and the enduring cycle of their intertwined fates.

Their journey led them into a vast desert where remnants of an ancient city lay buried beneath shifting sands. Local lore spoke of Zarath, a revered warrior king who had ruled the city millennia ago with wisdom and strength. Legend recounted how Zarath had wielded a blade infused with the power of the Heart of Aether, using its mystical energies to defend his people against shadowy invaders.

Intrigued by these legends, UNKNOWN THE SLASHER and his companions explored the ruins, guided by weathered inscriptions on crumbling walls. Deep within a hidden chamber, they uncovered murals and stone carvings that recounted Zarath's valiant stand against the encroaching darkness. His tale spoke of sacrifice and resilience, of a leader who had given everything to protect his city and people. Standing in the solemn silence of the chamber, UNKNOWN THE SLASHER felt a kinship with Zarath's unwavering determination. They departed from the ruins with a renewed sense of purpose, determined to honor Zarath's memory and ensure that his sacrifice was not in vain.

Their journey then led them to the verdant valleys of Aeloria, where they encountered tales of the Moonlit Order—a secretive group of warriors who had defended the realm during the Time of Shrouds, an era cloaked in perpetual twilight due to the absence of the moon. The Order's leader, Lady Elara, was renowned as a formidable sorceress who had harnessed starlight to erect a protective barrier against encroaching darkness.

In a secluded glade nestled within the lush forest, UNKNOWN THE SLASHER and his companions discovered a shrine dedicated to Lady Elara. There, they encountered an elderly guardian, one of the last remaining members of the Moonlit Order. The guardian recounted the Order's history, detailing Lady Elara's mastery of celestial magic and her relentless pursuit of the Heart of Aether—a relic she believed held the key to restoring balance and banishing darkness from the realm.

Tragically, Lady Elara's quest had remained unfulfilled as she perished in the final battle, her essence transcending into stardust that still shimmered in the glade. As the guardian spoke, UNKNOWN THE SLASHER and his companions felt the weight of Lady Elara's legacy upon them. They pledged to continue her mission, to seek out the Heart of Aether and to confront the lingering darkness that threatened their world.

Armed with the knowledge and determination gleaned from these ancient tales, UNKNOWN THE SLASHER and his companions pressed onward. Their quest for the Heart of Aether had taken on a deeper significance, fueled not only by the desire to defeat darkness but also to preserve the stories and legacies of those who had fought before them. Each step forward was a testament to their commitment, their journey a pilgrimage through history and myth in pursuit of a future bathed in light and peace.

As UNKNOWN THE SLASHER and his companions ventured deeper into their quest for the Heart of Aether, they arrived in the ancient forests of Eldoria, a realm where the Elves dwelled amidst towering trees and serene glades. The Elves, known for their long lifespans and profound connection to nature, held within their memories countless tales of epochs past. Among these legends, they recounted the harrowing saga of the First War of Shadows—a cataclysmic conflict that had nearly torn their world apart. It was during this turbulent era that a hero named Arion had emerged, wielding the fabled Heart of Aether to seal away a primordial darkness that threatened to engulf all existence. The Elves believed that Arion's spirit endured, guiding those who sought the relic with protection and sagacity.

Moved by their reverence for history, the Elven elders presented UNKNOWN THE SLASHER with an ancient map, purportedly drawn by Arion himself. Though time had weathered its markings, obscuring some details, it offered the best clues yet to locate the elusive artifact they sought.

Continuing their journey, they ascended into the northern highlands where legends whispered in the winds spoke of forgotten battles and the valor of lost heroes. In a secluded village nestled amidst rugged peaks, they encountered an elderly blacksmith who claimed lineage to Thalor, a renowned warrior of the Second War of Shadows. Thalor was famed for crafting weapons of unparalleled might, using shards of the Heart of Aether to imbue them with the power to dispel darkness. The blacksmith shared with them Thalor's journal—a testament to his ancestor's deeds and a map revealing the location of a hidden forge where the Heart of Aether could potentially be reforged into a weapon of ultimate potency.

With each revelation, UNKNOWN THE SLASHER and his companions realized that their quest transcended mere conflict. They were integral parts of a vast tapestry woven with threads of light and shadow, each thread representing the struggles and sacrifices of heroes long gone. Their journey now carried the weight of honoring these legacies while confronting the present darkness that threatened their world.

Following the ancient map and Thalor's detailed journal, they faced myriad challenges. Treacherous mountain passes tested their endurance, dark magic-twisted creatures lurked in their path, and labyrinthine caves concealed secrets and dangers alike. Each trial not only hardened their resolve but also deepened the bonds of camaraderie among them, forging unbreakable alliances rooted in trust and shared purpose.

One evening, as they rested beneath a starlit sky, UNKNOWN THE SLASHER spoke with solemn reverence, reflecting on the profound significance of their odyssey. "Our journey is intertwined with the echoes of those who came before us—Zarath, Elara, Arion," he mused, his voice echoing with conviction. "Their courage and sacrifices are our guiding light. We carry their legacy forward."

His companions nodded in silent agreement, their eyes reflecting determination and unwavering resolve. They understood that their path forward would be fraught with peril, yet they drew strength from the spirits of the past that guided them and the hopes of a brighter future that beckoned them onward.

With the ancient map as their compass and Thalor's journal as their guidebook, UNKNOWN THE SLASHER and his companions awakened the next morning with renewed vigor. They knew that every step brought them closer to the ultimate confrontation—a battle that would not only decide the fate of their world but also affirm their roles as custodians of a legacy spanning millennia.

Their journey through history had bestowed upon them a

profound understanding of their mission. They were not merely warriors seeking to confront present darkness; they were torchbearers tasked with safeguarding a heritage that transcended time. Armed with this realization, they pressed onward, resolute in their quest to locate the Heart of Aether and fulfill their destiny.

Made in the USA
Columbia, SC
19 November 2024

97b4a93e-f7ce-4d7c-949b-dcdac9987362R02